Through My Window

Other books about Jo and her family

Wait and See
In A Minute

For Islington Library Staff

Other books about Jo

Wait and See
In A Minute

Through My Window

Tony Bradman and Eileen Browne

MAMMOTH

Jo was ill in the night.
In the morning she had a temperature
and her dad said
she would have to stay indoors.

She wanted her mum
to stay at home, too.
But she had to go to work.

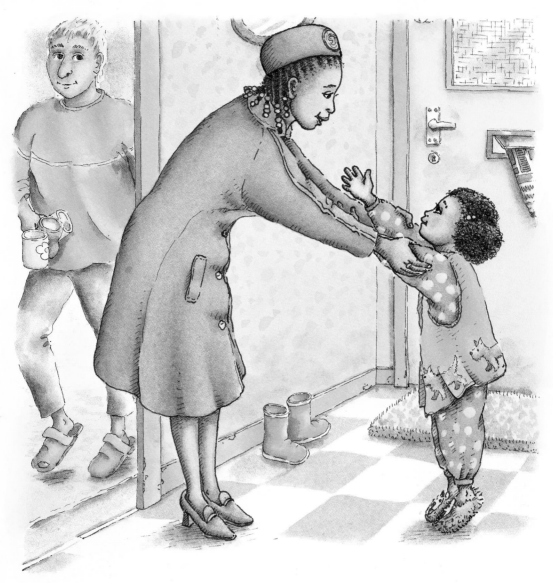

"Never mind, Jo.
Keep an eye out for me tonight –
I'll bring you a surprise
to make you feel better."

So Jo waved goodbye
to her mum
from the window
until she turned the corner
of the street.

Jo felt tired,
so she had a sleep.

When she woke up,
she heard feet
coming up the street.

Was it her mum
coming home
with her surprise?
She looked out
of the window.

But it was only Jo's friend,
the postman.
He waved, but he didn't have
any letters for Jo's flat today.

Jo looked at some books.
After a while she heard feet
coming up the street again
and a clinking,
clanking sound.
Was it her mum
coming home
with her surprise?

She looked out of the window.
But it was only her friend,
the milkman.
"Hello, Jo," he called,
and left some milk
outside their door.

Jo's dad brought her lunch
on a tray.

When she'd finished,
she heard some more feet
coming up the street.

Was it her mum coming home
with her surprise?
She looked out of the window.

But it was only her friend,
Mrs Ali, who lived next door.
"I've brought you some comics,"
said Mrs Ali,
and came in to see her.

Jo looked at the comics
and then she heard some barking
in the street.
Was it Jo's mum coming home
with a surprise that barked?

She looked out of the window.
But it was only Patch,
Mrs Ali's dog,
chasing a cat across the road.

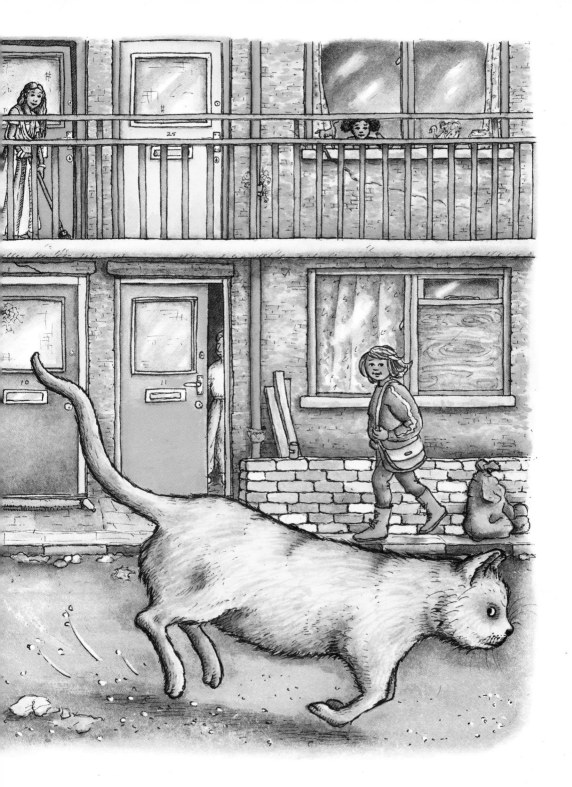

Jo felt tired
so she had another sleep.
She dreamed about all the things
her mum might bring her
as a surprise.

Then she dreamed that she could
hear feet in the street again,
and woke up.
Was it her mum coming home
with her surprise?

She looked out of the window.
But it was only her friend
the window cleaner.

The window cleaner
pressed her face
against the glass
and made Jo laugh.

But soon Jo was fed up.
Her mum would be ages yet.
And she'd probably forget
all about her surprise, anyway.

Jo heard some more feet
coming up the street.
They were coming closer,
and closer, and closer.

Was it Jo's mum coming home
with her surprise?
Jo looked out of the window.

Yes it was!
She ran down the hall
and opened the door for her mum.

"Here you are, Jo.
Here's a present
to make you feel better."

Jo opened the box.
And can you guess
what was inside it?

That's right –

the present she'd always wanted!

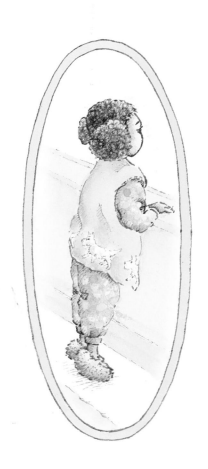

First published in Great Britain 1986
by Methuen Children's Books Ltd
Magnet edition published 1988
First published 1989 by Mammoth
an imprint of Reed Consumer Books Ltd
Michelin House, 81 Fulham Road, London SW3 6RB
and Auckland, Melbourne, Singapore and Toronto

Reprinted 1990, 1991, 1992 (twice), 1993 (twice),
1994 (three times), 1995

Text copyright © 1986 Tony Bradman
Illustrations copyright © 1986 Eileen Browne

ISBN 0 7497 0161 7

Printed in Great Britain
by Scotprint Ltd, Musselburgh